MY AMERICA

A Fine Start

Meg's Prairie Diary

· Book Three ·

by Kate McMullan

Scholastic Inc. New York

Kansas
1856

December 26, 1856

A new diary from Mother! It is my favorite Christmas gift. I am lucky to have it, as paper is scarce here in Kansas Territory — otherwise known as K.T.

Paper must be scarce in St. Louis, too. My friend Julia sent me a cross-written letter. First she wrote a page. Then she turned the page sideways and wrote across her writing.

Julia wrote that when she passes our old house in St. Louis, she misses me. It is nice to be missed. She wrote of tea parties in her parlor. And of evenings singing around the piano. Last summer her letter would have made me

homesick for St. Louis. But now K.T. seems more like home.

I must write back to Julia. I will cross-write, too. For I have so much to tell! I will tell how our friend Dr. Baer watched over Pres and me on a steamboat from St. Louis to K.T. And how Mother, Father, and Grace came to K.T., too. How we live in a small cabin with my Aunt Margaret and my three cousins. How my father and my uncle fought in a war to make K.T. a free state that does not allow slavery. How my uncle was captured by pro-slavery soldiers. How he is still in prison! How my father was shot in the shoulder. And how he is mending now. How I have learned to knit. And how, now that the war is over, I hope to go to school.

Aunt Margaret said we must have a happy Christmas even though Uncle Aubert could not be home. And we did. All of us children found penny candy in our stockings. It was great fun to see everyone open the gifts I made for them. Pin cushions for Aunt Margaret and Mother. Knitted wool mufflers for Father and Uncle Aubert. I knit one for my cousin George, too. He turned thirteen last week. So I made him the same gift as the grown men. I stitched small U.S. flags for my brother, Pres, and for my cousins, Charlie and John. I made a corn-cob doll for my sister. Grace named her Tess. I even made a yarn cat toy for Mouser.

Pres made no presents for anyone. He is only seven. So no one expected much. But he wrote a poem for Uncle Aubert. After Christmas dinner, he read it aloud to us. It was short and went like this:

"When you get home from prison, Uncle, dear,
We all will be so glad.
I will let you hold my snake,
The only one I ever had."

As Pres read, Aunt Margaret put her face in her hands. I thought she was sobbing. Then I saw that she was trying so very hard not to laugh.

December 27, 1856

So cold! Too cold to leave the cabin except to do the chores. Too cold for my friend Lily to ride Honey over to visit me. I miss Lily. I wish I could show her the flannel night-dress that Aunt Margaret made me for Christmas. It has three shell-shaped buttons. If only I had a pony, I would brave the cold and visit Lily.

Later

I asked Mother if school was going to start soon. And she told me that no place has been

 6

found yet in Lawrence for a new school. Don't people here know how important a school is?

December 29, 1856

The cold and wind let up today. Aunt Margaret drove the wagon to Lecompton to visit Uncle Aubert in prison. She took him food for a late Christmas dinner. And she took him his gifts.

I spent the day making candles with George. We built a fire in the yard and stood a great three-legged kettle over it. I put in hard fat called "tallow." It came from a neighbor's hogs. While the tallow melted over the fire, Grace helped me tie candlewicks to a stick. We set the stick over a tray of candle molds so that a wick went down to the bottom of each one. When the fat was melted, George ladled

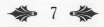

hot tallow into the candle molds. We left them to cool. Once they cooled, we lifted them out by their wicks. Now we have candles to light the long winter nights.

Making candles reminded me of making bullets. I have made both now. I much prefer making candles.

I still have the bullet that Dr. Baer took out of Father's shoulder. Sometimes I take it out of my trunk to look at it. Such a little thing. But it nearly killed Father. He still cannot lift his left arm. I am worried about him.

Later

Aunt Margaret is back. She said Uncle Aubert was happy to have the warm muffler I knit for him. She said Pres's poem cheered Uncle Aubert and the other prisoners. Pres looked proud to hear it.

 8

December 31, 1856

I bundled up to go to the barn to milk Mollie. The cold was so fierce it made my teeth ache. At least milking does not take long. Poor George. He has been out hunting all day in this awful cold.

Father is restless inside the cabin. I think he feels bad for not helping George bring in meat to feed us. Sometimes I see him trying to lift his injured arm. He makes a face, as though it hurts him terribly.

Later

What a fine surprise! In spite of the bitter cold, Dr. Baer picked up Miss Peach and Hannah Peach and drove them to our cabin. Dr. Baer brought an apple cake that he baked himself. It was delicious.

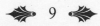

How good to see Hannah Peach! Because of our time together on the steamboat, I feel that she is my friend. I forget that she is sixteen and I am only nine.

When Hannah first came here from the vegetarian community, she was pale and thin. But now she is her pretty self again. She said the just-built cabin she shares with her aunt is warm and snug. She has lined the walls with blue paper. She said Lily's big brother, Theo, comes to split wood and do outside chores nearly every day. As she told me this, her face got pinker and pinker. Can Hannah Peach be falling in love with Theo? Wait until I tell Lily!

After we ate, Aunt Margaret got out her tambourine. Dr. Baer, Miss Peach, and Hannah began singing "Call to Kansas." I remembered how I first heard it sung on the steamboat, *The Kansas Hopeful*. I joined in singing:

*"We'll sing upon the Kansas plains
The song of liberty."*

Aunt Margaret says she has high hopes for 1857.

January 1, 1857

Before he left last night, Dr. Baer looked at Father's shoulder. He told Father to try to move his arm each day. Oh, I hope that will help him!

January 6, 1857

Pres is upset. The black snake he calls Jake is missing. Father says Jake is curled up sleeping through the winter. He says come spring, Jake will be back.

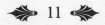

January 8, 1857

The cold is terrible. The wind blows snow through cracks in the cabin walls. This morning Grace and I woke up dusted in snow. My head hurts. My throat, too. First I am hot. Then shivering cold. I would like to curl up and sleep until spring like Jake the snake.

January 27, 1857

Now I know what it is like to have the ague. Otherwise known as the K.T. shakes. I have not been able to sit up for three weeks. Or write a single word in my diary. Mother says I was so hot and shook so badly I scared her near to death. I do not remember any of it.

Pres read me a poem he wrote for me. It went like this:

"Tomorrow is my birthday, Meg,
I am turning eight.
But if you still have the K.T. shakes,
You can give me a present late."

Pres turned eight last Tuesday. I slept right through his birthday.

January 28, 1857

Mother made a seat for me by the window. Mouser is curled up in my lap as I write. I can see Father trying to split wood with his good arm. Often, the log falls off the chopping block. Father keeps his left arm tight to his side. I wonder, can he move it at all?

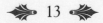

January 29, 1857

Mother and Aunt Margaret helped me stand today. My legs wobbled badly. It wore me out.

Later

The wind is howling like a pack of wolves. We shiver even inside the cabin. Tonight, Father gathered us around the fire. He read aloud from *A Midsummer Night's Dream*. He changed his voice for each character and made us all laugh. In this way, Father and Mr. Shakespeare warmed us on this cold winter's night.

January 30, 1857

Mr. Young, the traveling photographer, came to visit and stayed for supper. Afterward,

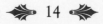

we sat around the fire. I was knitting. Mr. Young began telling a story. It had something to do with women going to saloons and breaking all the whiskey bottles. I was most eager to hear this story. But Mother shooed us up to bed, so I never found out why those women smashed the whiskey bottles.

January 31, 1857

Snowed all day. So quiet. Not long ago I went to sleep to the sounds of Border Ruffians firing off their guns. Now I feel safe. If only Uncle Aubert were home. If only I could go to school. Then K.T. would be fine.

February 2, 1857

It warmed up some and Lily rode over to visit me! I told her how Hannah Peach's face turned pink when she talked about Theo coming to help her and her aunt with chores.

Lily's eyes grew wide. She said, "So *that* is where he has been!"

She told me that Theo gets up extra early these days. He does his chores. Then he rides off. Everyone thinks he is out hunting. Lily says she will not tell anyone what I told her.

Then Lily told me wonderful news! The basement of the Lawrence Unitarian Church is being turned into a school. Lily's big brothers, Theo, Will, and Sam, are helping to build it. Lily says Judge Josiah Quincy of Boston sent money for the school. It will be called Quincy High School.

When she said that, I nearly burst into tears.

"You are eleven," I said. "You can go to high school. But I am only nine! I cannot go!"

But Lily says the school is for anyone from nine to twenty. So I *can* go!

Lily's mother's baby will come soon. She asked if I have been praying for a baby girl. I said I had. Lily asked me to pray all I can. Her six brothers are praying for another boy. We are badly outnumbered in our prayers.

Later

I felt a lump in my bedding. I reached under my quilt and discovered my Christmas candy! I hid it there from Pres. Then I forgot about it. I have ten pieces left.

February 5, 1857

Mother gave me some white wool. She showed me how to make baby booties by knitting two small squares and stitching the

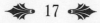

edges together. I am knitting little booties for Lily's baby sister.

Tonight, Father tried to help George clean his rifle. But he could use only one hand, and he dropped the gun. Father picked it up and handed it to George. Then he walked out of the cabin without saying a word.

Later

I lie in bed, awake. I can hear Mother and Father talking downstairs. I think they are talking about Father's arm.

February 7, 1857

Mother was rolling dough this morning. I asked her about Father's arm. She kept rolling. She said many are worse off. That was all she would say.

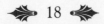

February 9, 1857

I helped Father hitch Bay to the wagon. He rode out to our claim. He says we have to build a cabin on it soon or we will lose it. That is the law. If you stake a claim, you must build a cabin on the land. It must measure at least twelve feet by fourteen feet.

I watched Father drive off. How can he build a cabin with one arm? Uncle Aubert could help. But he is in prison. What if we lose our claim? We will have no place to live. Aunt Margaret says she likes her cabin "full to bursting." But we cannot live here forever.

Later

The sky is dark. Snow is coming down fast. Father is not back yet. I am so worried. Hurry, Father!

Later

It grew so dark we lit candles mid-afternoon. Oh, how glad I was when Father burst through the cabin door. He was soaking wet from the snow. But he is home and safe. Under his good arm he carried a · bundle wrapped in a quilt.

Father is standing by the fire now. I asked him about the claim. I asked what was inside the quilt. But Mother shooed me away. She said Father must warm up before he answers any questions.

Later

A claim jumper has been on our land! Father said the claim jumper put up a cabin. A twelve by fourteen cabin.

20

"So fast?" said Pres.

Father nodded. Someone was trying to take away our land! But why was Father smiling?

Father said, "Would you like to see the cabin?"

"Now?" I said. "In the snowstorm?"

"Yes," said Father. "Now."

He asked Pres to carry over the bundle. Pres set it on the floor. Father unwrapped the quilt. And there stood a tiny cabin.

"It is twelve by fourteen," said Father. "Twelve by fourteen *inches*."

The cabin was made of sticks, not logs. It had a door. And two windows. It was a perfect little cabin!

Father told us that this is a trick. A claim jumper sets a little cabin down on a claim. Then he and a witness go to the Land Office. The claim jumper says the land should be his, for he has put up a twelve by fourteen cabin. And the witness can swear that this is the truth.

Grace said the little cabin would make a fine home for Tess, her corn-cob doll. Father said he thought so, too.

February 11, 1857

Father rode to Dr. Baer's claim today. I asked to go with him. But he said no. He said it firmly. I dared not ask a second time.

Bedtime

Father came home late. Pres, Grace, and I ran to greet him. But he barely said a word to us. His thoughts seemed far away.

Now Mother and Father are talking downstairs. I cannot hear what they are saying.

But they sound serious. I only hope Father will not go away again.

February 12, 1857

At dinner, George said he met Sam Vanbeek in the woods, hunting. Sam said that the new baby is here.

My heart began beating with excitement.

"Is it a baby girl?" I asked.

"No," said George. "A boy, Stewart."

A boy? After all those prayers!

Poor Lily. Seven brothers.

February 16, 1857

I cut my finger chopping carrots today. I could not sit still to stitch. Every time I moved, I bumped into someone. Tonight, when Father read from *A Midsummer Night's Dream*, all

the characters got mixed up inside my head. I thought maybe I was coming down with the K.T. shakes again. But Mother says it is only cabin fever. She says she has a touch of it herself from being too long in a small cabin.

February 18, 1857

A wonderful day!

Mother and Father took Grace, Pres, and me on an outing. We bundled up against the cold. I put on all my petticoats and my silk dress. Then my prairie dress. And my coat on top of both. Aunt Margaret wrapped me in her double shawl. In the wagon, we snuggled under buffalo robes. Only my nose was cold. As we went, Bay's breath made clouds in the frosty air.

Father says a dose of town is a known cure for cabin fever, so we drove first to Lawrence. I thought everyone might be inside in such freezing weather. But the streets were filled with people. Father said many of them are emigrants.

"Are what?" said Pres.

"Emigrants," said Father. "People who came from someplace else to live in Kansas. People like us."

Mother told us that the Gold Seekers' Trail goes right through Lawrence. This trail begins in the east and leads all the way west to California.

Lawrence has grown since the last time I was there. There are fewer tents now. And more log cabins. More brick houses, too. The Free State Hotel is being rebuilt. Uncle Aubert will be so glad when he hears this!

Father stopped the wagon on Henry Street in front of an empty house three stories tall. Father said it is a "ready-made house." It was built in Ohio. As soon as it was finished, the

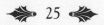

house was torn down. It was brought to Kansas in pieces and put up again. There is a little barn out back. Father seems quite taken with this house.

Next, we drove to the Land Office. On the way, we passed the Unitarian Church. This is where Quincy High School will be! I tried my best to see if any work was going on in the church basement. But I saw no sign of it. Does that mean it is finished? And that school will start soon? I hope so!

When we reached the Land Office, Father went inside. He said he had to do something about our claim. We waited for him in the wagon. To help pass the time, we played "I Spy." It kept us from feeling the cold.

Father came out at last and we headed home. On the way, we stopped at the Vanbeek's cabin to see baby Stewart.

Lily held her baby brother to show him to

us. He is very red in the face. "I know you did your best, Meg," she said. "But those boys out-prayed us."

I gave Lily the booties I made. Lily unwrapped the bottom of Stewart's blanket to put them on. Oh, I never knew feet could be so small. The booties I made would fit a baby giant! They are way too big for little Stewart. But Mrs. Vanbeek says if he is like her other boys, he will soon grow into them.

Mother gave Mrs. Vanbeek a pot of stew to feed her family. Then she held the baby and got all teary. I know she was thinking of the two baby boys she lost to cholera.

February 23, 1857

Aunt Margaret looks worn out from her long trips to the Lecompton prison. But Uncle Aubert needs the food, clothes, and blankets

she takes to him. George wants to go in her place. But he is our hunter. We need the game he brings us each day.

February 24, 1857

Lily rode over and jumped off Honey while the pony was still moving. I feared something awful had happened. But Lily was only in a hurry to tell me the most wonderful news. Theo asked Hannah Peach to marry him. And Hannah said yes! They will be married on April 19.

Lily said she had to get home to help with the baby. She jumped back on her pony and trotted off. I never did get to ask her about Quincy High School.

Oh, Hannah Peach, a bride! If only I had a pony, I would ride out to her claim and hug her.

February 25, 1857

I am knitting a scarf for Mother. As I knit I worry. Can Quincy High School have started without me?

February 28, 1857

This morning I glanced out the window. I saw a boy riding a pony toward our cabin. He looked about George's age. He was leading another pony behind.

Mother was fixing dinner. "Go see what he wants, Meg," she said.

I put on my coat and mittens. I went outside.

The boy stopped his pony. I did not know him. But I knew the pony he was leading. It was Sally!

Sally had been my pony for one day. Uncle

Aubert bought her for me from Mrs. Biggs. I tried to ride Sally. But I could not steer her. She always trotted straight back to Mrs. Biggs's barn. Uncle Aubert had to come and get me. Mrs. Biggs gave him his money back. And that was the end of my pony.

"I am Adam Cook," the boy said. "Are you Meg?"

I said I was.

"My grandmother is Mrs. Biggs," said Adam. "She asked me to bring Sally to you."

"Oh, dear," I said. "Has your grandmother gone to her heavenly reward?"

"No," said Adam. "But she is going to California."

California!

He said that Mrs. Biggs has had enough of K.T. winters. She has packed up her things. As soon as a suitable wagon train comes through this spring, she will join it, going west.

I thanked Adam. But I said I could not make Sally turn, so she could not be my pony.

"You can turn Sally," said Adam. "Before you pull on the reins, just say, 'Sugar!'"

Adam boosted me up onto Sally's back. I tried his trick. It worked! Sally turned every time.

Adam and I took Sally to the barn. I fed her some hay. Good old Sally!

Mother asked Adam to come inside and warm up. She gave him a cup of coffee with hot milk. I quickly wrote to Mrs. Biggs. I thanked her for the pony. And told her good luck in California!

March 1, 1857

March winds are blowing hard.

I asked Mother if I might ride Sally to visit Lily. She said I may go if the wind lets up.

 31

Aunt Margaret will not let the wind stop her. She drove to Lecompton again this morning with a food basket for Uncle Aubert.

Later

The wind let up enough for me to ride to Lily's cabin. Sally turned every time I said "Sugar!"

I found Lily in the barn. She was so surprised to see me! She said her mother needed some peace. That is why she was looking after two of her little brothers in the barn. It was warm there with all of us and the animals.

Lily says Quincy High School has not started yet. First the weather was too cold for the workers. Then snow melted and flooded the church basement. So the work is not finished. Oh, it is hard to wait!

Hannah Peach and Miss Peach came to

supper at Lily's cabin last week. Lily loves Hannah. She says maybe she does not have a little sister. But soon she will have a big sister — Hannah Peach.

Later

I am sorry that Lily has no little sister. But I am not so happy about her new big sister. I know it is wrong of me to feel this way. But I wish Hannah Peach were going to be my big sister, not Lily's.

March 2, 1857

It is dark out. Aunt Margaret is not back from Lecompton. Mother is uneasy.

March 3, 1857

Mother sat mending by the cabin window all morning. She kept a look out for Aunt Margaret. Suddenly she cried, "My heavens!"

I was knitting and nearly dropped all my stitches. I ran to the window. Bay was pulling the wagon toward the cabin. Aunt Margaret sat in the driver's seat. But who was that, all bundled up next to her? And then I saw. It was Uncle Aubert!

We all rushed out to welcome him home. He has been gone eight months. Five of them he spent in prison. Oh, how good to have him with us again! He is very thin. But he is in good spirits. And so happy to be home.

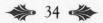

Later

After supper, Uncle Aubert asked George to walk with him out to the barn. When they came back, George looked pleased. I think Uncle Aubert must have told him what a fine job he did while he was away.

March 5, 1857

It has warmed up! The snow is melting. Now we have mud. Mud, mud, mud. When I went out to the barn, I sank up to my ankles.

After chores I rode Sally to the Peaches' claim. The mud was awful. Sally got stuck twice. I had to slide off her back and pull her foot out of the mire. By the time I reached the claim, I was muddy all over.

But Hannah Peach hugged me as if I did

 35

not have a speck of mud on me. How good to see Hannah Peach!

Hannah had been chopping potatoes. I sat down to help her. As we chopped, I asked how she came to be engaged to Theo. Hannah's face turned pink. And she told me the most wonderful story.

Hannah keeps a journal, just as I do. She said she often wrote about Theo Vanbeek. About what a fine man he is. How he cares for his family. How he helps his neighbors. How he came, day after day, to help build the Peaches' cabin. How she admires him.

One freezing cold day, Theo came over to help the Peaches with chores. Afterward, Miss Peach invited him to come in and warm himself before he headed home. Then she said she must attend to some things in the barn. So Hannah and Theo were left alone. Theo noticed Hannah's journal on a table near the

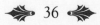

fire. He said he would rather read that book than anything by Mr. Shakespeare. Hannah's face grew quite pink as she told me this. She said she did not know what made her so bold, but she picked up her journal, opened it to where she had last written of Theo, and she read the passage out loud. She said when she finished, Theo was smiling. He said her words had warmed him more than any fire could. And he asked her to marry him!

I thought about Hannah and Theo as I rode home. I was so deep in happy thoughts that I forgot to say "Sugar." By the time I collected myself, Sally and I were halfway to Mrs. Biggs's barn!

March 6, 1857

Mother and Father drove to Lawrence today. When they came back, I asked what

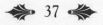 37

they did in town. Mother only smiled. What can they be up to?

March 9, 1857

Mother and Father got ready to drive to Lawrence again. Mother said when they came back, they would have news.

I sat by the window, knitting, the whole time they were gone. Pres hovered near me. Grace kept saying, "Are they back yet? Are they back yet?"

At last we caught sight of them. All three of us ran to meet them. Mother stopped Bay and we jumped into the wagon.

"Tell them, Duncan," Mother said to Father.

Father smiled. "Over dinner," he said.

Pres and Grace raced into the cabin. They set the table. Pres dished out the meal. Grace

carried plates to our places. Aunt Margaret said she never knew they could be such good help.

At last we sat down. Uncle Aubert said grace.

We looked at Father.

"Well?" said Pres.

"A one-armed man cannot farm," said Father.

I gave a little cry. "You have two arms!" I said.

Father shook his head. "We must face the truth, Meg," he said. "I cannot lift my left arm. I went to see Dr. Baer. My arm is as mended as it is going to get."

I frowned. I did not like thinking of Father as a one-armed man.

"That is the bad news," Father went on. "But I have good news, too."

"What? What? What?" we all cried.

Father smiled. He told us that when he went to the Land Office, he signed his claim over to the claim jumper. Then he asked around about the ready-made house. He found out that it belonged to a Mr. Stuben from Ohio. Mr. Stuben brought his family to K.T. during the war, just when the Border Ruffians tried to attack Lawrence. Mr. Stuben said he did not want to live in such a dangerous place. So his family packed up and went back to Ohio. That is why the house is empty.

"A one-armed man can run a business," said Father. "So your mother and I have bought the ready-made house. I will open a store on the ground floor. I will sell supplies to emigrants in K.T. And to folks headed west. We will live over the store in the ready-made house."

I gave a whoop of joy. We will live in town. And close to school! It will be almost like living in St. Louis.

But Grace did not whoop. She said she did not want to leave her cousins. Or Mouser. Pres did not whoop, either. He said soon Jake would wake up. He felt sure that his snake would not want to live in town.

Mother said, "Jake will like the barn out back."

Pres darted me a look. He could not believe it. Mother was so happy she was not thinking clearly. She was going to let him take the snake!

Father said when the weather warms, we will pick up our furniture from the storehouse in Leavenworth. And we will take it to the ready-made house.

Uncle Aubert said he is happy we will have our own home. And happy that we will be so near. Cheery Aunt Margaret surprised me by saying that she feels sad. Sad that this time of being together is coming to an end. I feel sad about that, too.

 41

March 20, 1857

A windy morning. After chores, I rode Sally to the Peaches' claim. I had to tell Hannah our news.

When I got there, the Peaches were eating dinner. Dr. Baer was there. So was Theo Vanbeek! The men had come to plow the Peaches' fields. Hannah was very pink and happy.

Hannah gave me a plate of baked squash and apples. I said it was very good. Theo said he thought so, too. For a vegetarian dish. He gave me a wink. Hannah said one day Theo will make a fine vegetarian.

Then I told our news about the ready-made house. Everyone was so happy for us. Theo is a fine carpenter. He says that house is very well built.

After dinner, Hannah walked me out to the barn to get Sally. She talked about the wedding. It will be at their claim. Reverend Still from the Blue Mound Sabbath School will perform the ceremony. Dr. Baer and Miss Peach will do most of the cooking. Hannah says the redbud should be out by April 19. She will carry redbud as her bouquet.

Then Hannah told me something so sad. She said that five years ago, her mother, father, and two sisters died in a terrible fire. She was visiting her aunt, Miss Peach, at the time. That is why she was not killed with them. She said now, as she plans her wedding, she misses her family more than ever. Tears came to her eyes as she spoke. I reached out and hugged her. Poor Hannah Peach! Then in a shaky voice Hannah said that I am the closest she has to a sister out here in K.T. She asked if I

would wear a sprig of redbud at the wedding to show I am her almost sister. Tears sprang to my eyes. Happy, sad tears.

"Of course I will be your sister for the wedding, Hannah," I told her. "I will be your sister always. So will Grace. So will Lily. Now you have three Kansas sisters."

Hannah smiled through her tears.

I feel bad that I did not want Hannah to be Lily's big sister. Now I hope they will be true sisters forever.

I cried all the way home.

March 23, 1857

At last! School is about to begin! Will Vanbeek rode by our cabin today to give Uncle Aubert some seeds. He says he and his crew have finished putting up the blackboards. He says the teacher has arrived. She is

 44

boarding with a family in Lawrence. Her name is Miss Lucy Wilder. I wonder what she is like.

School! I have not seen India or Louisa since we all hid from the Border Ruffians on Blue Mound. But I will see them soon at school!

March 25, 1857

The weather has warmed. Father is going to Leavenworth tomorrow to pick up our furniture. There is a whole house full of it. So he has hired two teams and two large wagons. Now that Uncle Aubert is back, George can be spared to drive the second wagon.

Later

Father asked me to go to Leavenworth with him and George. He says he has one good arm. And he needs me to take the place of the

other. I am glad to help him. I only hope Quincy High School will not begin while we are gone.

March 26, 1857

Father woke me before dawn. Brrr! It felt like winter again. Mother packed us a hamper. Father, George, and I had just started off when one of our wagon wheels broke. It was nearly noon by the time Uncle Aubert fixed it. At last we set off. George drove one wagon. I sat on the seat beside Father and drove the other.

Now we have stopped to eat our dinner. I believe Father thought warm weather was here to stay. But it is cold. Too cold to write another word.

Later

Here we are at the Fish Hotel. It is owned by a Shawnee named Pascal Fish. It is packed with families on their way to Lawrence.

We arrived after dark. My arms ached from holding the reins. I have never been so hungry. We went straight to the dining room. I am writing as we wait for a table. I hope we get one soon!

March 27, 1857

We finally got our turn to be fed last night. Afterward, we got our bedding from the wagon. Pascal Fish's little daughter, Eudora, showed us to our room. We were surprised to find that it was also the room of some two dozen others! There was one bed and five chairs. But they were taken. Everyone else had

spread their bedding on the floor. There was hardly any space left. Father and George found empty spots on the men's side of the room. I stepped over many sleepers on my way to the ladies' side. At last I found a small empty place not too far from the fire. I was so tired, I fell right to sleep. When I awoke this morning, I found my head resting on another young lady's feet! She laughed and said she hoped they made me a fine pillow.

No more now. We are setting off again.

Leavenworth

Father and George have gone to see about our things. I am staying with the wagons. I do not like the look of the sky.

Later

A snowstorm blew in!

Father, George, and some hired men loaded our furniture onto the wagons. They covered it with tarpaulins. They wrapped ropes around the load and tied them tight. We had just set off for home when a howling storm hit. The spring snow caught everyone by surprise. Every traveler on the road began looking for shelter. We turned back to Leavenworth. The snow fell so thick we could hardly see. It took us some time to find a hotel. But at last the tiny Riverside Hotel took us in.

All five guest rooms in the hotel were filled. So we are camped in the lobby with many others. We are wet and cold. But Father says we must be thankful we did not perish in the storm.

Our horses are out back in the barn. The

wagons with our furniture are crowded in there, too. We are safe. That is all that matters. I must stop thinking about Quincy High School. And whether I am missing it.

Father says spring snows melt quickly. So we will be off tomorrow.

March 28, 1857

At last the snow has stopped. It comes up to my waist. It is not melting. We cannot leave the hotel. Father says others are worse off. I know he is right. But it is hard to sit still at the Riverside Hotel.

Later

George is helping to shovel a path from the hotel to the barn. Father says as soon as the path is finished, George and I may go and feed

the horses. And look in on the wagons. He is worried that snow may have seeped through the coverings and wet our furniture.

Here comes George. And here I go!

March 29, 1857

Father prayed aloud this snowy Sabbath morning. He gave thanks for our many blessings. Then we had silent prayers. I believe we all prayed for the same thing. Please, Lord, melt the snow!

Later

People are starting to leave the hotel. But Father says our goods are heavy. He does not want our wagons to get stuck in the mud. So we are waiting.

Later

And waiting.

Evening

We are the only people left at the Riverside Hotel.

March 30, 1857

Father took a walk this morning. He came back shaking his head. Too much mud.

George and I have played "I Spy" until there is nothing else to spy.

That is all I have to write in this diary.

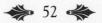

March 31, 1857

Off at last! Oh, but it was hard going. Melting snow dripped down on us from tree branches. The road was a mud wallow. We got stuck several times. We had to jump out and push the wagons. We became coated in mud. I got used to it. After a while, I didn't even mind.

Now we are back at the Fish Hotel. One good thing about the mud: There are not many people here. So we were first in line for dinner. Eudora Fish came and sat beside me as we ate. She told me she is five years old. I said I had a sister just her age. That seemed to please her.

April 1, 1857

We rose early. As we left the hotel, Eudora ran outside after us. She put something into my hand. It was a blue bead. It is the same size

as the shell-shaped buttons on my night-dress. Now I have a memento of the Fish Hotel.

We drove the furniture to Lawrence. Father hired some men to carry it into the ready-made house. Father returned one wagon. We drove the other to the cabin. We arrived after dark. Home at last! How good it felt to wash off all that mud.

Bedtime

Mother called up to the loft that Quincy High School will begin tomorrow. I had forgotten all about it!

April 2, 1857

George had many chores to do this morning. He told me not to wait for him. So I rode to Lily's cabin. Then the two of us

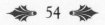

rode to Lawrence. We put Honey and Sally in the pony barn behind the Unitarian Church. Then we lined up on Ohio Street with the other scholars. I counted almost sixty in the line. Our teacher, Miss Wilder, led us into the building and down the stairs. And so Quincy High School began.

It is an elegant school. There is a bell. And a wall clock. In the rear of the room are settees made of shiny black walnut. Blackboards are built into the walls and circle the whole room. We have real desks, too. I never dreamed the school would be so fine. Thank you, Judge Josiah Quincy of Boston, for caring about a school for the children of K.T.!

Miss Wilder is small. She cannot be much older than Hannah Peach. She wears her brown hair in one thick braid wrapped twice around her head. I wonder how long her hair is.

India and Louisa came to school, too. They

introduced Lily and me to their friend Alice Bailey. She is twelve and very tall. Her hair is red, like mine. Lily's brothers Will and Sam were at school. And India's big brother Peter. George ran in just before the bell rang.

Adam Cook, who brought me Sally, came late. As a punishment, Miss Wilder said he must put his name on the blackboard. Adam picked up a stick of chalk. He began writing his name in big, looping letters. He took his time. We all looked on, wishing we could be the first to write our names on that beautiful blank blackboard instead of Adam Cook. It was not much of a punishment.

Then Miss Wilder taught us about digestion. She said we must chew each bite of food twenty times before we swallow.

Later

I tried chewing like Miss Wilder said at supper tonight, but kept losing count.

April 3, 1857

Louisa brought a "charm string" to school today. She showed it to us at recess. It is a most wonderful thing — buttons all strung together on a length of strong thread. Louisa's has sixty-seven buttons! The idea is for friends to give buttons to one another for remembrance. And for good luck. When the charm string rattles, it makes the loveliest sound.

Later

I have started my own charm string. Mother gave me sixteen buttons from her mending kit. Three are from a worn-out blue shirt of Father's. Aunt Margaret gave me seven buttons. That makes twenty-three! On Monday, I will trade some of them to Louisa.

Later

I had the best idea! I wrote to Julia in St. Louis. I told her about charm strings. I sent her six buttons to start one of her own. Now I have only seventeen buttons left. But I hope Julia will send me some buttons.

April 6, 1857

Mother and Father have been working hard to get the new house ready for us. Tomorrow is moving day! I am packing my things.

Pres is moody. He says he will not go

without his snake. Father told him that our new next-door neighbor, Mr. Butler, rents out space in our barn to keep an enormous fat sow named Mae. That cheered Pres some.

Today Miss Wilder read to us from a book called *Lizzie's Many Failings*. In the first story, Lizzie's little brother Herbert had a terrible runny nose. But Lizzie did not share her handkerchief with him. This meant she was Selfish.

Pres often has a runny nose. Why do boys never carry their own handkerchiefs?

Later

Grace asked me to make her a charm string. I gave her five buttons from my own string. My string is now only twelve buttons. I feel very Unselfish.

 59

Later

Tonight after supper, Aunt Margaret grew teary. She said she would miss us. That she liked her cabin full to bursting. Her tears were contagious. We all cried and hugged and cried some more. Mother said it was silly. We are moving only five miles away. But she said it with tears running down her cheeks.

April 7, 1857

I slept in Lawrence last night, in my old St. Louis bed. Oh, how good it felt! The window of my room overlooks the street. I can see everyone who passes by.

Our bedrooms are on the second floor of our house. The third floor is still empty. Pres says he could raise snakes up there. All

different kinds of snakes. Mother says she is sure we can think of a better use.

Mother sat down at the piano this morning and played. She says she hopes a piano tuner will soon move to Lawrence.

Off to school!

Later

I have come home for dinner. Children who live in town do this. But I miss eating dinner at school with Lily, India, Louisa, and Alice.

As we ate, Pres recited a new poem for me. It goes like this:

"In the barn there lives a pig.
She is not small. But she is big.

Her name is Mae. She is a sow,
And not a horse or goat or cow."

I told Pres he was improving.

April 8, 1857

Miss Wilder was late to school today. We were all seated when she walked into the room. She went right to the blackboard and wrote her own name as a punishment! I like Miss Wilder.

Alice Bailey has a charm string as long as my arm! She says it has almost 400 buttons. She went to visit her aunt in Topeka and it turned out that her aunt had worked as a seamstress. She had a box full of buttons and she gave them all to Alice. Lucky, lucky Alice.

Louisa is most unhappy. Once she had the longest charm string. Now hers is shorter

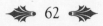

by hundreds of buttons. I have twenty-two buttons now. I added the blue bead from Eudora Fish, which makes twenty-three. It is not so many. But I know where each one came from.

Lily was not in school today. I hope she is not sick.

Bedtime

Tonight after supper, Mother sighed. She said she feels we are rattling around in our big new house. I have been feeling the same way. I miss Aunt Margaret so much. I never thought I would miss being crowded all together, but I do.

April 9, 1857

It rained hard last night. This morning everyone tracked mud into our beautiful

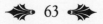

schoolroom. One good thing came of the mud. Mother did not want me tracking any more than necessary into our new house. So she gave me my dinner to eat at school.

Lily was not sick yesterday. She went with a Quaker group to visit the Lawrence School for Negro Children. She said they did sums that were much harder than anything Miss Wilder has given us.

April 10, 1857

Mother says I may take my dinner to school every day!

Miss Wilder read to us again from *Lizzie's Many Failings*. This story told how Rose had a pony to ride to school. Lizzie wished she had the pony instead of Rose. Lizzie's new failing is Envy.

Alice Bailey's charm string is now nearing 500 buttons. I am trying hard not to have the failing of Envy myself.

Later

Pres dragged me out to the barn. I did not want to go. But I am so glad I did! For in the night, Mae gave birth to a litter of fourteen spring piglets. I have never seen anything sweeter than those little pink pigs.

April 11, 1857

Lily rode to visit me today. We put Honey in the barn next to Sally. I showed her the piglets. Then the two of us walked all over town. It was exciting to see so many different kinds of people. We passed two Delaware

Indian women dressed in beautiful beaded leather. And behind them came a Negro man carrying a bag of carpenter tools. Then came a woman in a blue dress with a big hoopskirt. She carried a blue parasol to shade her face from the sun and held the arm of a man with a moustache and a stove-pipe hat. Right behind them came a group of men all in buckskin. They were chewing big wads of tobacco and spitting it right on the street.

April 13, 1857

Miss Wilder let us have a spelling bee today. We put our toes to a line on the floor. We stood straight, with good posture. Miss Wilder went down the row, giving us words to spell. My heart began to pound. I was so afraid I would not know how to spell my word.

 66

India's big brother Peter stood next to me. His word was "suppose." He did not know how to spell it. So he had to sit down at his desk. I felt bad for him, for he is almost as old as the teacher. I had to take his word. I must have spelled it right, for Miss Wilder did not tell me to sit. We went on for several more rounds. I was lucky and stayed in the bee. Lily stayed up, too.

Each round, Miss Wilder gave harder and harder words. George missed "achievement" and sat down. Lily went down on "encouragement." I went down on "aggravate." But by that time I did not mind so much.

The last one standing was Alice Bailey. She is only twelve. Yet she out-spelled all the older scholars. Alice Bailey has no Failings.

April 14, 1857

Uncle Aubert, Aunt Margaret, George, Charlie, and John came for supper. They brought one of Mother's baby apple trees. Uncle Aubert dug a hole and planted it beside our ready-made house. He says soon it will give shade and apples.

They brought another present, too. Jake the snake! One sunny day last week, he crawled out from the sod in the summer kitchen. Pres hooted with happiness. Then he and John took the snake to his new home in our barn.

April 15, 1857

Every day before school, Pres and I hoe our side yard to make a garden. Soon we will plant

vegetables and flowers. Miss Wilder told us that the air we breathe out our noses is very good for plants. I plan to breathe all I can on our garden.

April 16, 1857

Grace came to supper holding her charm string. It was long! I asked where she had gotten so many buttons. But she would not say. At bedtime, I tried to put on my night-dress. But the buttons were gone. I went to find Mother. Her nightdress was missing its buttons, too. We went to find Grace. We asked to see her charm string. And there were our buttons. Grace confessed that she took Mother's scissors from her sewing box. And she cut buttons off every piece of clothing she could find. Even from her own dresses. I am now

helping Mother sew the buttons back on. Grace is helping, too. Mother says if she can use scissors so well, it is time she learned to use a needle.

April 17, 1857

Pres, Mother, and I planted our garden. We put in green beans, corn, rhubarb, carrots, potatoes, squash, pumpkin, onions, watermelon, berries, and lettuce. And flowers. Lots of flowers.

Father is his old whistling self again. Every day he gets shipments of things to sell to emigrants who come to K.T. And to folks in wagon trains going west.

Later

Oh, no! Dr. Baer stopped by. He said Reverend Still has come down with the K.T.

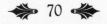

shakes. He is out of his head with fever. He is far too sick to marry Hannah and Theo. Will their wedding be called off?

April 18, 1857

The wedding is saved! A circuit preacher rode in to Lawrence last night. He stopped to water his horse in front of the Emigrant Aid Society. Mr. Vanbeek was there, working. He saw the preacher and ran outside. He asked him if he would marry Hannah and Theo. The preacher agreed. His name is Reverend Biddle.

I helped Aunt Margaret make an apple pie for the wedding supper. It is baking now. Mmm, the cinnamon smells so good. Mother is making corn pudding.

April 19, 1857

Oh, my! What a wedding! I will never forget it as long as I live. Too tired to write about it now.

April 20, 1857

Miss Wilder says that if we want to tell a story, we must start at the beginning. So that is what I will do.

It was a bright sunny day. And not much wind.

I put on my prairie dress. And my sunbonnet. I helped Grace get dressed. Then we all drove to the Peaches' claim. As we drew near, we met other wagons on the road. Everyone was going to the wedding.

Dr. Baer greeted us when we drove up to the claim. We hopped out of the wagon. Will

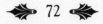

and Sam Vanbeek took our horses to the barn. I carried our basket of food over to a pic-nic table.

There must have been 100 guests at the wedding. Everyone was talking and laughing. The men looked handsome in their straw hats. Many of the Vanbeek's Quaker friends came to the wedding. They wore dark clothing. Mr. Young, the traveling photographer, came, too. So did many students from Quincy High School. Miss Wilder was there. And Alice Bailey. Mrs. Biggs's daughter came. And her ten children, including Adam. I saw one of Lily's brothers holding little Stewart. He has grown so big since I last saw him. (But his feet still look too small for the giant white booties.) Miss Peach pointed out two friends of Hannah's from the vegetarian community. They drove all night long to come to her wedding.

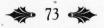

An old gentleman sat on a stool in the shade of the cabin. He was very large. His buttons looked as if they might pop off at any moment. He held his wide-brimmed hat in one hand. With the other, he mopped his forehead with a handkerchief. I wondered who he was.

Hannah hurried over to me. She was pinker than ever. She had on a pale blue calico dress with a wide lace collar. She had dried flowers in her hair. She looked so beautiful. Hannah pinned a small clump of redbud to my dress.

"There!" she said. "Now you are my sister!"

She gave me a hug.

Lily ran over to us. Hannah pinned redbud to her dress, too. I felt so glad that Hannah and Lily would be sisters. Lily said the redbud made us sisters, too.

Soon, Miss Peach and Dr. Baer began

asking people to move to the little hill behind the cabin. We all gathered there, standing in a semicircle. Then the very large man huffed and puffed his way up to the top of the hill.

"Dearly beloved," he said in a deep, booming voice. Now I knew who he was, Reverend Biddle.

Hannah and Theo stood before him.

Reverend Biddle spoke about the happy state of marriage. He recited Bible verses by heart. He recited Psalms. He told how best to raise children. He boomed on for some time. He seemed to forget he was there to marry Hannah and Theo. At last Theo cleared his throat. This sound brought Reverend Biddle back to his job and he began the wedding ceremony. Theo and Hannah said their vows. Then Reverend Biddle pronounced them husband and wife. When the bride and groom kissed, Hannah turned as pink as a spring piglet!

Everyone thought the wedding was over. But Reverend Biddle was only just warmed up.

"Who else will come up the hill and be married?" the preacher boomed. "Come! All ye who will embrace this chance to be happily wed!"

Reverend Biddle seemed to forget that this was only Hannah and Theo's wedding.

"Young couples!" he called. "Step up! Let me join you in marriage! Only half the usual fee!"

Everyone murmured. No one knew what to do.

Then Dr. Baer spoke up. "Young couples only, you say?"

"Come one, come all!" cried Reverend Biddle. "Any age couple will do!"

Then to the astonishment of all, Dr. Baer looked at Miss Peach and said, "This is as good a time as any. What do you say, Miss Peach?"

And Miss Peach said, "Amen to that."

Then the two of them marched to the top of the hill and stood before Reverend Biddle.

"Make it a fast one," said Dr. Baer. "We are not getting any younger."

In less than a minute, Dr. Baer and Miss Peach were married.

Later, Dr. Baer told us that he and Miss Peach were planning to marry quietly the next week. But, he said, here was a chance not to be passed up.

Hannah and Theo will live in the Peaches' just-built cabin. And Dr. Baer and Miss Peach — I mean, Mrs. Baer — will live in Dr. Baer's cabin.

After the ceremony, we feasted on roasted turkey and rolls and butter. And potatoes and carrots and cakes, pies, and apple jellies. We feasted until we could not hold another bite.

Only Reverend Biddle kept going. He ate and ate long after everyone else had stopped. I

 77

began to hope that his buttons really might pop off. I badly wanted one for my charm string to remember him by.

After the dishes were cleared, Mr. Vanbeek tuned up his fiddle. Hannah and Theo and others their age formed up for a dance. Next came the quadrille. Dr. Baer and the new Mrs. Baer danced this one. So did Mother and Father. After that we all joined in and what a merry time we had.

We danced and sang until the stars came out. When it was time to go, Mother spread quilts in the wagon bed. Pres, Grace, and I climbed in. We snuggled up all together. We rode home, looking up at the wide prairie sky.

April 21, 1857

Mr. Young stopped by our house. He showed us the photographs he took at Hannah

and Theo's wedding. There was one of Hannah, Lily, Grace, and me. I told Mr. Young I thought it was a most beautiful picture.

Mr. Young had some good news. He is setting up a studio on Indiana Street in Lawrence. He says many wagon trains will be passing through this summer. Travelers want likenesses to send to their families back east. So he expects to make a fine living.

April 22, 1857

Miss Wilder says we may no longer bring our charm strings to school. She says we rattle them and disturb everyone.

April 30, 1857

On my way to school this morning I saw the first green shoots coming up in our garden!

 79

To think such tiny plants will grow to feed us in the fall.

May 4, 1857

A letter from Julia arrived. A letter filled with buttons! She says she started a charm string with the buttons I sent. Now all the girls at my old school have them. And they all sent me buttons. Julia told who had sent each one. As I slipped them on to my charm string, I pictured each friend's face. I feel like the richest person on earth.

May 5, 1857

Alice showed us a new game today called "Drop the Handkerchief." We all stood in a circle. Alice skipped around the outside. She

held a handkerchief in her hand. As she skipped she dropped the handkerchief behind India. Then she began to run around the circle. India picked up the handkerchief and ran after Alice, trying to tag her. But Alice made it back to India's place before she was tagged. Then it was India's turn to skip around the circle. We had such fun!

May 7, 1857

Miss Wilder read us another chapter in *Lizzie's Many Failings*. Today, Lizzie spent all her money on a beautiful pin for herself. In this one act, Lizzie committed three Failings. She showed Vanity. And Selfishness. Lizzie also turns out to be a Spendthrift.

I am growing fond of Lizzie. What will she fail at next?

May 11, 1857

A twister is coming! I am so frightened!

We studied all morning in the schoolroom. The wind was howling. But that is nothing new for Kansas.

At noon, we stopped for recess. We lined up at the rear door. Adam Cook pushed on the door. The wind caught it and blew it wide open. He tried to run outside. But the wind was so strong it blew him back inside.

"I saw a twister!" he cried.

I looked out the door and saw it, too. A huge, dark, funnel-shaped cloud against the sky.

Miss Wilder was very calm. She told us to go back to our desks. Then she tried to close the door. She managed to step outside. But she could not pull the door shut. Some of the big boys ran to help her. We were all frightened. But we had to laugh when Miss Wilder came

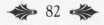 82

back inside. All her hairpins had been blown away! Her hair looked as wild as the wind.

Miss Wilder told us that in a tornado, a basement is the safest place in the world. Now she is reading to us from *Lizzie's Many Failings*. She must shout to be heard above the wind. But I cannot listen. Not even Lizzie can keep me from aching with worry for my family. Mother and Father will take Pres and Grace to the basement of the ready-made house. But what about Aunt Margaret and Uncle Aubert, out there on the prairie? Will they be safe? George's face is very tight. Alice Bailey is crying. I feel like doing the same. If the twister touches down, it will be awful! Writing in my diary helps to calm me. At least a little.

Later

The wind has died down. Miss Wilder has closed the book. She will lead us outside now. What will we find?

Later still

We came up the stairs and out to the street. What a surprise to find a blue sky. And the sun shining! Everything was still. There were no people. Bricks and lumber had blown into the streets. Windows had broken. But no houses were knocked down. Thank goodness!

I hugged Lily. And George. Then they and the other prairie children ran to the barn to get their ponies. They were galloping home before I had run one block.

On my way home I passed Father! He was

going to check on our neighbors. I reached our house and Mother hugged me. I felt her trembling. She is so worried about Aunt Margaret.

I asked Mother to let me ride to Aunt Margaret's cabin to make sure that everyone is safe.

But Mother shook her head. "No, Meg," she said. "It is too dangerous for you to go."

Later

I am going to Aunt Margaret's cabin. I have to! Mother does not know how to ride a pony. Father is not here. And I cannot stand not knowing. Neither can Mother. I must go.

George was forgiven for going to Blue Mound with the flag that time. I hope I will be forgiven, too.

May 12, 1857

I was so frightened riding out on the prairie. Nothing looked the way it used to. The wind had blown prairie grass over the path. I could not always tell where I was. Many trees had blown down. I passed the place where the lightning-struck oak had stood. All that was left was a jagged stump. My heart pounded the whole time, knowing how upset Mother would be when she found me gone.

Sally took me on down the road. At last I caught sight of the little cabin. I let out my breath. It was still there!

But I was glad too soon. For as I got closer, I saw that the cabin had no roof! And where was the barn?

"Sugar, Sally!" I said. "Faster!" She picked up her speed. When we got close, I jumped off

her back and ran into the cabin. Everything had blown upside down. But there was Aunt Margaret. She was folding quilts. She was as cheery as ever.

"Meg!" she said, smiling. "We've lost our roof. But we are fine."

My legs wobbled. I had to sit down right on the floor. I was so relieved to hear it!

"What about Mollie?" I said. "And her calves? And Kip and Bay?"

"We all went down to the stream," Aunt Margaret said. "Aubert tied the animals to trees. We all hunkered down and hoped the wind would not find us. And it did not." Then she added, "But I have not seen Mouser."

Oh, poor little gray cat. Blown away.

I told Aunt Margaret that I had to go right back to Mother. That she did not know I had come.

Aunt Margaret nodded. "Go on," she said. Then she called after me, "Meg? Tell your mother to get ready for company!"

Later

I am forgiven. Mother hugged me tight when I returned. She wept with relief to know her sister and her family are safe.

May 13, 1857

I am crying so hard I can hardly write. Will Vanbeek is dead! He was trying to save their horses in the storm. He was struck on the head by a tree branch and killed instantly. Oh, poor Will. Poor Lily!

Mother has never been on a pony. But I helped her up onto Sally's back. She rode right to the Vanbeek's cabin to take food and

comfort to Mrs. Vanbeek. I gave Mother my charm string to give to Lily. I want her to have it to let her know her "sister" is thinking of her.

Losing Will is the saddest news. But there is more that is bad.

Hannah and Theo went down to their root cellar to wait out the storm. When they came out, they found that their just-built cabin had blown away. They have gone to live with the Baers.

Alice Bailey's cabin also blew away. They lost everything. Even her charm string is gone. To think, all those buttons, blowing in the wind.

May 14, 1857

We drove to the Vanbeeks's claim for Will's burial. The sky was as gray and looked as sad as we all felt, standing in a circle around his grave. I held Lily's hand while she wept.

Later

Aunt Margaret, Uncle Aubert, George, Charlie, and John arrived this evening. And Mouser. The cat had only been hiding. They brought their bedding and moved onto the third floor.

"Now *our* house is full to bursting," said Mother.

Pres says he would rather have his cousins live upstairs than a whole nest of snakes. Mother says she could not agree more.

Mollie and her calves and Kip, the ox, and Bay have moved into the barn with Mae and Sally. Now the little barn is full to bursting.

So much terrible sadness and so much happiness, all in the same day.

May 15, 1857

My birthday! It snuck up on me, I have been so busy. To think, I am ten years old.

On my last birthday, I went for ice cream at the Barnum's City Hotel in St. Louis. That seems so long ago.

Mother and Father gave me a gift at breakfast. He bought a likeness from Mr. Young. It is the one from Hannah Peach's wedding. It shows Hannah, Lily, Grace, and me. Mr. Young titled it "Four Sisters." It is a treasure.

Grace gave me a present this year. Two buttons to start a new charm string. She had to promise many times that she did not cut them off anyone's clothes. She says Minnie Butler next door gave her the buttons.

Pres did not give me a present I could open. He gave me a poem. It goes like this:

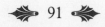

"Happy birthday to you, Meg.
I hope you never break your leg,
Or break your arm or get a blister.
I love you, Meg, my best big sister."

My birthday is off to a fine start.

Life in America
in 1856

Historical Note

Settlers traveled to Kansas Territory in the 1850s by train, covered wagon, or oxcart. Many of them were seeking a place to live where there was no slavery. Some settlers came from free states in the east, where slavery was not allowed. They looked forward to voting in K.T. to make sure it became a free state, too. Other settlers came from southern states where people owned slaves. Many of these settlers had their hearts set on raising their families out from under the

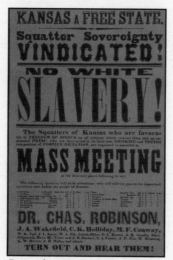

Poster advertising Kansas as a free state.

Voting in Kansas.

shadow of slavery. But no matter where they came from, none of the settlers expected to face the vicious fighting of the border wars, where free-staters and pro-slavery armies clashed. The Civil War did not officially break out until 1861, but in 1856 in Kansas Territory, the fighting had already started.

The battle for Kansas.

Governor John White Geary.

In the late fall of 1856, when Governor Geary sent the Border Ruffians back to their home states, most of the fighting ended. Peace was declared, and with the coming of spring, Lawrence turned into a "boom town." Emigrants from the east rushed to Kansas to stake claims of land. Houses sprang up. Wagon trains on their way to California or Oregon often stopped in Lawrence to buy supplies. The Free State Hotel was rebuilt and called the Eldridge Hotel.

Many K.T. settlers, like Meg's father, saw the opportunity for opening businesses in Lawrence. Some Native Americans, Shawnee and Delaware, saw the opportunity, too. A few, like Pascal Fish, opened hotels. Others, like Chief Bluejacket, operated ferry services across various rivers.

Native Americans meet with the U.S. Commission in Kansas.

Not everyone who came to K.T. was American. Settlers came from Europe, too. In 1857, a group of Germans came. They stayed at the Fish Hotel. When they set up a town of their own nearby, they named it Eudora, after Pascal Fish's five-year-old daughter.

Staking a claim of land in Kansas Territory was not an exact science. There were no reliable maps, and few fences. A boundary might be established by counting how many times a wagon wheel rolled over a given distance. By law, anyone who staked a claim was required to build a twelve-by-fourteen-foot cabin on the land. That was the only way he could hold the claim. But before he got around to building a cabin, a settler might "stake" a claim by hammering three wooden stakes into the ground, forming a "tripod." These stakes, called "straddle-bugs," were respected as a promise that a cabin would be coming soon.

Settling Kansas.

Construction of a cabin.

Building a cabin was not easy on the Kansas prairie. Trees were scarce. Settlers took turns helping one another raise cabins. Sometimes land speculators looked for ways around the regulations. They might put miniature cabins on the land that measured twelve by fourteen *inches*! There were other methods of fooling the Land Office officials, too. One was a cabin that truly measured twelve by fourteen feet. But it was built on wheels so it could be pulled from claim to claim by horses or oxen. Kansas Territory was a land of many opportunities. It was the beginning of the "Wild West."

About the Author

Kate McMullan says, "I turned ten in 1957, exactly 100 years after Margaret Cora Wells would have turned ten, in 1857. It was such fun to imagine what life might have been like a century before I was born and to write Meg's story set in that time. It was also fun to name many of the characters in Meg's diaries after my relatives — my Aunt Grace and Uncle Aubert, my father Lee and his twin brother, Larry, my Uncle Pres, my niece Margaret, my nephews George, Charlie, John, and Stewart, and to imagine them as settlers in K.T. during this exciting time in American history."

Kate McMullan has written more than

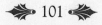

fifty books for children, including the best-selling *If You Were My Bunny* and *The Story of Harriet Tubman, Conductor on the Underground Railroad*. Her recent *I STINK!* a monologue by a garbage truck, was illustrated by her husband, the noted illustrator Jim McMullan, and was the recipient of a 2002 *Boston Globe–Horn Book* Honor and was voted one of the Ten Best Illustrated Books of 2002 by *The New York Times Book Review*. Kate lives with her husband, their daughter, two cats, and a dog in New York City and Sag Harbor, New York.

For Judith M. Sweets,
with enormous gratitude

Acknowledgments

The author would like to thank her editors, Beth S. Levine and Lisa Sandell, for their encouragement and inspiration. She would also like to thank Judith M. Sweets of the Douglas County Historical Society, Lawrence, Kansas, whose felicitous research provided the author with so many wonderful voices of the brave and hopeful K.T. settlers, especially the charming thirteen-year-old Maggie Harrington, who kept a journal in 1867.

Grateful acknowledgment is made for permission to reprint the following:

Cover Portrait by Glenn Harrington
Page 95: Kansas Free Soil poster, North Wind Picture Archives, Albert, Maine.

Page 96 (top): Voting in Kansas, Copied from Richardson's *Beyond the Mississippi*. Courtesy of the Kansas State Historical Society, Topeka, Kansas.

Page 96 (bottom): Battle for Kansas, Lithograph of the Battle of Hickory Point drawn by W. Breyman. Courtesy of the Kansas State Historical Society, Topeka, Kansas.

Page 97: Governor John White Geary, Getty Images, New York, New York.

Page 98: Native Americans with U.S. government officials, from *The Illustrated London News*. Courtesy of the Watkins Community Museum, print from the Kansas State Historical Society, Topeka, Kansas.

Page 99: Settling Kansas, by J. E. Rice of Lawrence, Kansas. Courtesy of the Kansas State Historical Society, Topeka, Kansas.

Page 100: Building a cabin, Getty Images, New York, New York.

Other books in the My America series

Corey's Underground Railroad Diaries
by Sharon Dennis Wyeth

Elizabeth's Jamestown Colony Diaries
by Patricia Hermes

Hope's Revolutionary War Diaries
by Kristiana Gregory

Joshua's Oregon Trail Diaries
by Patricia Hermes

Meg's Prairie Diaries
by Kate McMullan

Virginia's Civil War Diaries
by Mary Pope Osborne

Copyright © 2003 by Kate McMullan

All rights reserved. Published by Scholastic Inc.
SCHOLASTIC, MY AMERICA, and associated logos are trademarks
and/or registered trademarks of Scholastic Inc.

Library of Congress Cataloging-in-Publication Data
McMullan, Kate.
A fine start: Meg's Diary / by Kate McMullan
p.   cm. — (My America; Meg's prairie diary; bk. 3.)
ISBN 0-439-37061-2; 0-439-37062-0 (pbk.)
I. Title.   II. Series.
2002044580
CIP AC

10 9 8 7 6 5 4 3 2   06 07

The display type was set in Rogers.
The text type was set in Goudy.
Photo research by Amla Sanghvi.
Book design by Elizabeth B. Parisi.

Printed in the U.S.A.   23
First edition, August 2003